Will, you were the inspiration for this adventure.
I love you to the moon, the stars, to Mars, and back.

Jim, this book would have never come to life without you.
All my love and thanks.

D1410734

Poem, illustrations, and design copyright © 2014 by Jennie Turrell
All rights reserved.

No part of this book may be reproduced, stored in a retrieval system, or transmitted in
any form or by any means, electronic or mechanical, including photocopying, recording,
or otherwise, without the written permission of the publisher.

Library of Congress Cataloging-in-Publication Data

A catalog record of this book is available from the Library of Congress.

ISBN 978-0-8192-2983-0 (pbk.)
ISBN 978-0-8192-2984-7 (ebook)

Illustrations and cover art by Jennie Turrell

Morehouse Publishing, 4785 Linglestown Road, Suite 101, Harrisburg, PA 17112
Morehouse Publishing, 19 East 34th Street, New York, NY 10016

Morehouse Publishing is an imprint of Church Publishing Incorporated.
www.churchpublishing.org

Printed in the United States of America

This book and its digital collages were compiled on an iMac® using Adobe® InDesign®
and Adobe® Photoshop®. The collage materials included felt, iPhone® photographs,
found objects, Will's handwriting, acrylic paint, and melted Crayola® crayons.
The background art and other painted elements were created on 98# Canson® XL® mix
media paper. The book was set with Kidprint®, Sabon®, and Myriad ® typefaces.

Let us pray

A little kid's guide to the Eucharist

Poem and pictures by
Jennie Turrell

Let's stand and praise God today.
Listen and look. Sing and pray.

The music starts. Time to sing.
Let God hear our voices ring.

As acolytes are passing by
let's watch the cross, held up high.

Watch the choir step two by two.
Hear the words? Can you sing too?

The Celebrant—last in line,
later blesses bread and wine.

Listen and look. Sing and pray.
Let's share the bread and wine today.

Blessed be God: Father and Son,
Holy Spirit, three in one.

Read aloud the words in *blue*.
They are here for me and you.

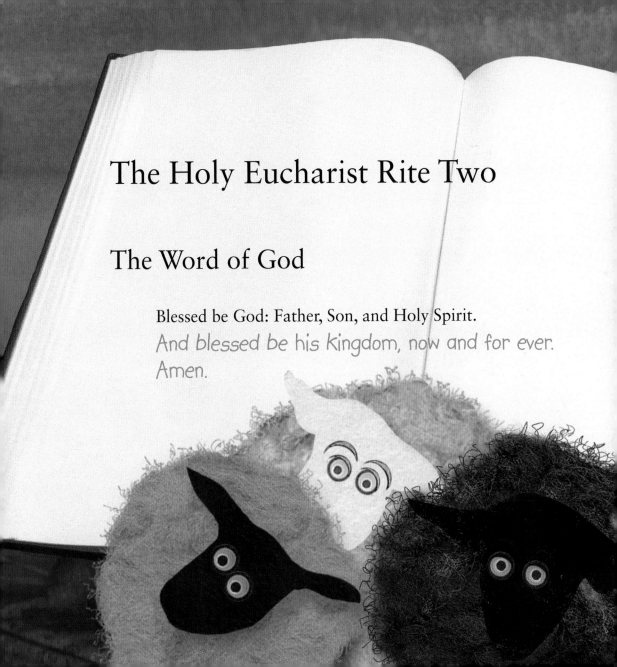

The Holy Eucharist Rite Two

The Word of God

Blessed be God: Father, Son, and Holy Spirit.
And blessed be his kingdom, now and for ever.
Amen.

Glory to God in the highest,
    and peace to his people on earth.
Lord God, heavenly King,
almighty God and Father,
    we worship you, we give you thanks,
    we praise you for your glory.

Lord Jesus Christ, only Son of the Father,
Lord God, Lamb of God,
you take away the sin of the world:
    have mercy on us;
you are seated at the right hand of the Father:
    receive our prayer.

For you alone are the Holy One,
you alone are the Lord,
you alone are the Most High,
    Jesus Christ,
    with the Holy Spirit,
    in the glory of God the Father. Amen.

On this day we gather here,
    asking God to please draw near.

    Gather all the prayers we pray
        for the Collect of the Day.

Listen and look. Sing and pray.
What's the lesson of the day?

Time for stories, read aloud
from the lectern, clear and loud.

Read the Gospel. Share it well—
over the hills and in the dell.

The Holy Gospel of our Lord Jesus Christ
according to _____.
Glory to you, Lord Christ.

The Gospel of the Lord.
Praise to you, Lord Christ.

The Sermon

Preachers walk us through the text.
How and why? What happens next?

We believe!

We believe!

We believe!

The Nicene Creed

We believe in one God,
    the Father, the Almighty,
    maker of heaven and earth,
    of all that is, seen and unseen.

We believe in one Lord, Jesus Christ,
    the only Son of God,
    eternally begotten of the Father,
    God from God, Light from Light,
    true God from true God,
    begotten, not made,
    of one Being with the Father.
    Through him all things were made.
    For us and for our salvation
        he came down from heaven:
    by the power of the Holy Spirit
        he became incarnate from the Virgin Mary,
        and was made man.

For our sake he was crucified under Pontius Pilate;
    he suffered death and was buried.
    On the third day he rose again
        in accordance with the Scriptures;
    he ascended into heaven
        and is seated at the right hand of the Father.
He will come again in glory to judge the living and the dead,
    and his kingdom will have no end.

We believe in the Holy Spirit, the Lord, the giver of life,
    who proceeds from the Father and the Son.
    With the Father and the Son he is worshiped and glorified.
    He has spoken through the Prophets.
    We believe in one holy catholic and apostolic Church.
    We acknowledge one baptism for the forgiveness of sins.
    We look for the resurrection of the dead,
        and the life of the world to come. Amen.

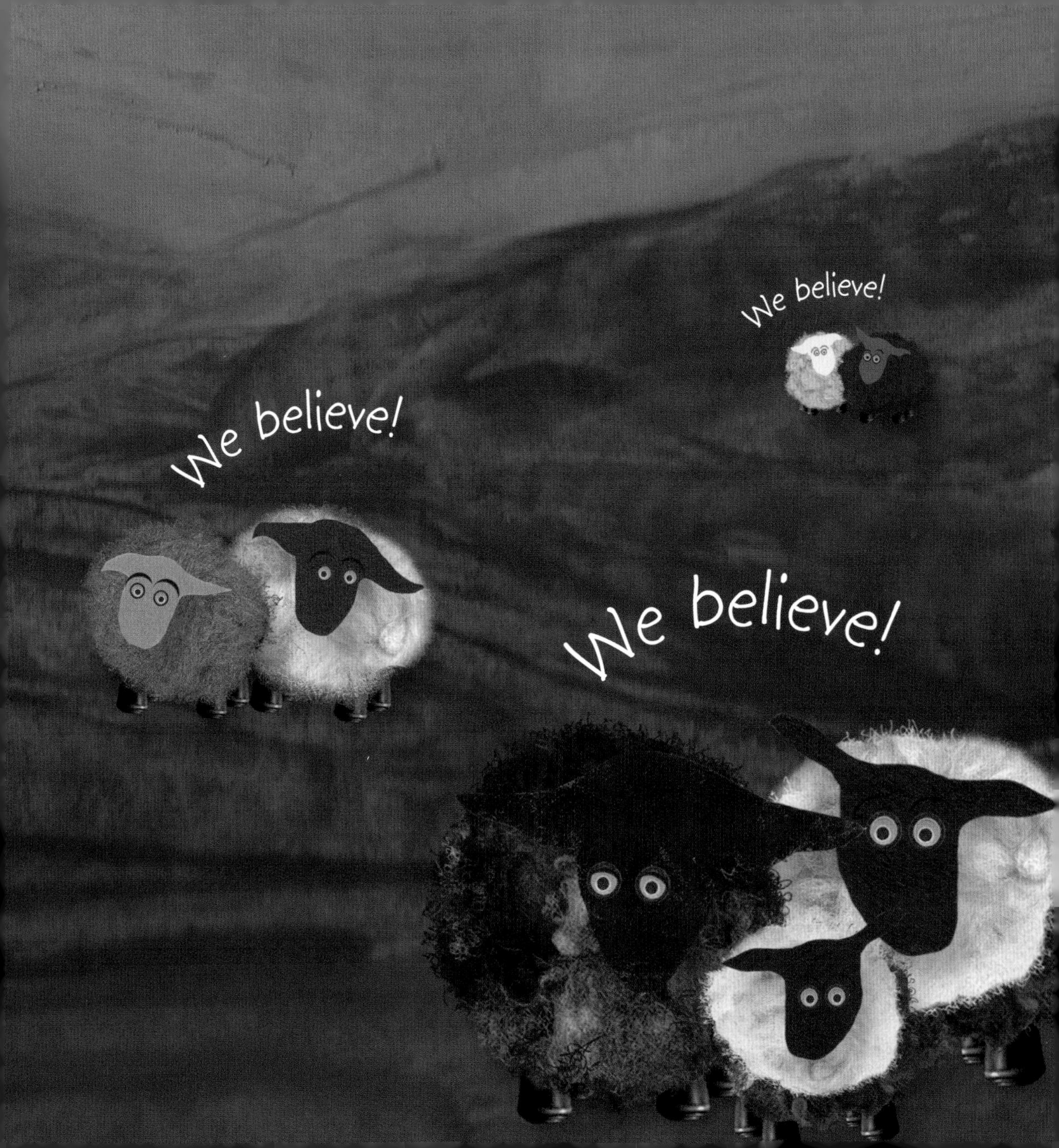
We believe!
We believe!
We believe!

The Prayers of the People

Form IV

Let us pray for the Church and for the world.

Grant, Almighty God, that all who confess your Name may
be united in your truth, live together in your love, and reveal
your glory in the world.
Silence
Lord, in your mercy

Hear our prayer!

Guide the people of this land, and of all the nations, in the
ways of justice and peace; that we may honor one another
and serve the common good.
Silence
Lord, in your mercy

Hear our prayer!

We pray for all on this earth
in their death and at their birth

and in between—hurt or sad.
God, please help when things are bad.

God loves this world, you and me,
birds in the air, fish in the sea.

Give us all a reverence for the earth as your own creation,
that we may use its resources rightly in the service of others
and to your honor and glory.
Silence

Lord, in your mercy

Hear our prayer!

Bless all whose lives are closely linked with ours, and grant that we may serve Christ in them, and love one another as he loves us.

Silence

Lord, in your mercy

Hear our prayer!

Comfort and heal all those who suffer in body, mind, or spirit; give them courage and hope in their troubles, and bring them the joy of your salvation.

Silence

Lord, in your mercy

Hear our prayer!

We commend to your mercy all who have died, that your will for them may be fulfilled; and we pray that we may share with all your saints in your eternal kingdom.

Silence

Lord, in your mercy

Hear our prayer!

Almighty and eternal God, ruler of all things in heaven and earth: Mercifully accept the prayers of your people, and strengthen us to do your will; through Jesus Christ our Lord. Amen.

Confession of Sin

Let us confess our sins against God and our neighbor.

Most merciful God,
we confess that we have sinned against you
in thought, word, and deed,
by what we have done,
and by what we have left undone.
We have not loved you with our whole heart;
we have not loved our neighbors as ourselves.
We are truly sorry and we humbly repent.
For the sake of your Son Jesus Christ,
have mercy on us and forgive us;
that we may delight in your will,
and walk in your ways,
to the glory of your Name. Amen.

Sometimes we hurt each other a lot.
There are things we can fix and things we cannot.

God is kind and will show us the way
to heal the hurt—

I'm sorry.

in God's time. In God's way.

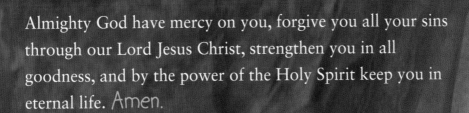

Almighty God have mercy on you, forgive you all your sins through our Lord Jesus Christ, strengthen you in all goodness, and by the power of the Holy Spirit keep you in eternal life. Amen.

The Peace

The peace of the Lord be always with you.
And also with you.

As we try to reconcile,
God stands with us all the while.

The peace of God, you will see,
helps us live in harmony.

Share God's love across the land.
All together—hand in hand.

Set the table. Watch and pray.
Let's share the bread and wine today.

The Holy Communion

The Great Thanksgiving

Eucharistic Prayer B

The Lord be with you.
And also with you.

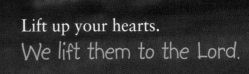

Lift up your hearts.
We lift them to the Lord.

Let us give thanks to the Lord our God.
It is right to give him thanks and praise.

It is right, and a good and joyful thing, always and everywhere to give thanks to you, Father Almighty, Creator of heaven and earth.

Because in the mystery of the Word made flesh, you have caused a new light to shine in our hearts, to give the knowledge of your glory in the face of your Son Jesus Christ our Lord.

Therefore we praise you, joining our voices with Angels and Archangels and with all the company of heaven, who for ever sing this hymn to proclaim the glory of your Name:

Holy, holy, holy Lord, God of power and might,
heaven and earth are full of your glory.
Hosanna in the highest.
Blessed is he who comes in the name of the Lord.
Hosanna in the highest.

We give thanks to you, O God, for the goodness and love which you have made known to us in creation; in the calling of Israel to be your people; in your Word spoken through the prophets; and above all in the Word made flesh, Jesus, your Son. For in these last days you sent him to be incarnate from the Virgin Mary, to be the Savior and Redeemer of the world.

In him, you have delivered us from evil, and made us worthy to stand before you. In him, you have brought us out of error into truth, out of sin into righteousness, out of death into life.

On the night before he died for us, our Lord Jesus Christ took
bread; and when he had given thanks to you, he broke it, and
gave it to his disciples, and said, "Take, eat: This is my Body,
which is given for you. Do this for the remembrance of me."

After supper he took the cup of wine; and when he had given thanks, he gave it to them, and said, "Drink this, all of you: This is my Blood of the new Covenant, which is shed for you and for many for the forgiveness of sins. Whenever you drink it, do this for the remembrance of me."

Therefore, according to his command, O Father,

We remember his death,
We proclaim his resurrection,
We await his coming in glory;

And we offer our sacrifice of praise and thanksgiving to you, O Lord of all; presenting to you, from your creation, this bread and this wine.

We pray you, gracious God, to send your Holy Spirit upon these gifts that they may be the Sacrament of the Body of Christ and his Blood of the new Covenant. Unite us to your Son in his sacrifice, that we may be acceptable through him, being sanctified by the Holy Spirit. In the fullness of time, put all things in subjection under your Christ, and bring us to that heavenly country where, with [_____ and] all your saints, we may enter the everlasting heritage of your sons and daughters; through Jesus Christ our Lord, the firstborn of all creation, the head of the Church, and the author of our salvation.

By him, and with him, and in him, in the unity of the Holy Spirit all honor and glory is yours, Almighty Father, now and for ever. AMEN.

And now, as our Savior
Christ has taught us,
we are bold to say,

Our Father, who art in heaven,
hallowed be thy Name,
thy Kingdom come,
thy will be done,
on earth as it is in heaven.
Give us this day our daily bread.
And forgive us our trespasses,
as we forgive those
who trespass against us.
And lead us not into temptation,
but deliver us from evil.
For thine is the Kingdom,
and the power, and the glory,
for ever and ever. Amen.

The Breaking of the Bread

Alleluia. Christ our Passover is sacrificed for us;
Therefore let us keep the feast. Alleluia.

The Gifts of God for the People of God.

The Body of Christ, the bread of heaven. Amen.

The Blood of Christ, the cup of salvation. Amen.

As we walk up to receive,
think about what we believe.

Let us pray.

Eternal God, heavenly Father,
you have graciously accepted us as living members
of your Son our Savior Jesus Christ,
and you have fed us with spiritual food
in the Sacrament of his Body and Blood.
Send us now into the world in peace,
and grant us strength and courage
to love and serve you
with gladness and singleness of heart;
through Christ our Lord. Amen.

The blessing of God Almighty, the Father,
the Son, and the Holy Spirit, be upon you this day,
and remain with you always. Amen.

Go in peace to love and serve the Lord.
Thanks be to God.